The Fangs, Vampire Spy, series

FANGS
VAMPIRE SPY

TARGET: NOBODY

TOMMY DONBAVAND

WALKER
BOOKS

First published 2013 by Walker Books Ltd
87 Vauxhall Walk, London SE11 5HJ

10 9 8 7 6 5 4 3 2 1

This book has been typeset in Helvetica and Journal

Printed and bound in Great Britain
by Clays Ltd, St Ives plc

British Library Cataloguing in Publication Data:
a catalogue record for this book is available from the British Library

ISBN 978-1-4063-3161-5

www.walker.co.uk

www.fangsvampirespy.co.uk

For Bryan and Bridget,
who first introduced me to Lindos

MPI Personnel

Agent Fangs Enigma
World's greatest vampire spy

Agent Puppy Brown
Wily werewolf and Fangs's super sidekick

Phlem
Head of MP1

Miss Bile
Phlem's personal
secretary

**Professor
Hubert Cubit,
aka Cube**
Head of MP1's
technical division

"And the award for the highest number of criminal *monster*minds arrested in the past year goes to … Agent Osiris Tut."

The audience in the ballroom of the Dorchester Hotel applauded as a mummy wrapped in crisp, white bandages made for the stage. Seated at a table near the front of the room, Special Agent Fangs Enigma took a deep drink of his blood-flavoured milkshake, his sharp vampire teeth rattling against the glass. "Well, that's another Spookie I haven't won. That one had my name all over it as well."

Fangs's date – a young woman called Skylar Ribble – gave him a consolatory cuddle. "Why would your mummy friend want that award if it's got your name written all over it?" she asked.

Sitting across from the pair was werewolf and spy Puppy Brown. She tried to hide her smile. "Osiris was always going to win that one, boss," she said. "He captured the entire Pink Pixie gang in one go last month – and there are over six hundred of them."

"Yeah, well, I could catch tiny pixies if I wanted to," grunted Fangs. "But I go after big villains instead. Big, mean villains who can do more than just nip you with their miniature teeth. And that selfless bravery has cost me an award."

"Well, I'm enjoying myself," said Puppy, taking a sip of her orange juice. "This is my first Spookie Awards ceremony since joining the agency." She and Fangs were both special agents at Monster Protection, 1st Unit, aka MP1. "It's great fun."

"I suppose it would be fun if you weren't expecting to win anything," said Fangs. "But I've got a reputation to think of."

On the stage, a green slime beast was slithering up to the microphone. It was Phlem, the head of MP1. He surveyed the assembled spies, lab technicians and security personnel in front of him. "Now to present the next award," he glugged, "please welcome Professor Hubert Cubit."

The crowd clapped as a man with a perfectly square head took to the stage. "Er … hello?" he said into the mike. "Many of you already know me as Cube, the head of MP1's technical division and all-round genius. This evening, however, I shall be *squaring up* to another challenge, that of presenting the award for the best use of a gadget in the field."

"This is the one," said Fangs, crossing his fingers.

"But you don't like Cube's gadgets," said Puppy. "You're always moaning about the equipment he gives us."

"That doesn't mean I'm not brilliant at using them."

"And the winner of the Spookie is … Agent Puppy Brown," Cube announced.

Fangs stared, open-mouthed, as the room erupted in applause. Puppy stood slowly and then made her way to the stage, where Cube handed her a golden statuette that was shaped like a ghost.

"What's this for?" she asked.

Cube smiled. "You cooked an omelette for Captain Shadow with the eggs I had injected with jellyfish DNA, causing him to glow in the dark. He was easy to locate and arrest after that."

Puppy stepped up to the microphone. "Thank you." She smiled. "But I was just doing my job – and getting to Captain Shadow would never have been possible without the help of my boss. So I'd like to dedicate this award to Fangs Enigma."

Fangs was on stage in a flash. He snatched the Spookie award from Puppy and then from his pocket he pulled a piece of paper with a prepared speech on it. "There are so many people I'd like to thank—"

Suddenly, there was an explosion, and the entire room was filled with black smoke. People collapsed to the ground with streaming eyes, coughing on the thick clouds. Puppy thought she saw shapes moving through the gloom – thin figures with stark, white limbs. Skeletons? She counted at least six of the creatures before they were lost in the smoke. Then she heard some unusual noises…

CRACK! CLICK! SNICK! SNAP!

In the darkness, Puppy fumbled to pull her phone from her utility belt.

"Lock the doors!" Phlem roared, trying to be heard over the noise of coughing, spluttering and screaming. "No one gets in or out."

Fangs searched about until he found Skylar. "Get under the table," he told her. "And keep my Spookie safe."

"*Your* Spookie?" spluttered Skylar. "B-But I th-thought…"

"Just look after it."

By the time Fangs had emerged from beneath the table, Puppy had hacked into the hotel's air-conditioning controls on her mobile and set everything running in reverse at full power. Gradually, the smoke began to disappear – and it wasn't the only thing to vanish…

"The skeletons have gone!" cried Puppy.

Phlem snatched the microphone from its stand with a slime-covered hand. "Is everyone all right?" he asked. "Check on the other MP1 personnel at your table. I want to know if anyone is hurt."

After a moment, Agent Tut joined Phlem on stage. "No injuries, sir," he reported.

"Good," said Phlem. "Agent Brown, get me the CCTV tapes for the entire hotel, inside and out."

"Yes, sir," replied Puppy.

"Agent Enigma, get out there and interview the hotel staff. Someone has to have seen who did this."

"I'm on it," said Fangs, taking a quick peek beneath the tablecloth to make sure both his date and treasured award were still there.

"Cube," Phlem said, "get back to the lab and

prepare for a full-scale investigation. No one attacks MP1 and gets away with it."

There was no reply.

"Cube … CUBE!"

"I don't think he'll be able to hear you, sir," said Puppy, a note of panic in her voice. "Cube is missing!"

TOP SECRET
MP1 Mission File #4
Target: Nobody
Report by: Agent Puppy Brown

The MP1 laboratory was full of white-coated technicians working late and yet it seemed strangely quiet without Cube. In fact, I couldn't remember a time when his square head hadn't been hovering somewhere in the background in here.

Early on in life, Professor Hubert Cubit realized that facts and information only ever come in square things. "Books, computers, filing cabinets – all square and all filled with knowledge," he once told me. "Tennis balls, potatoes and scoops of ice cream – all round and hardly any knowledge in them at all."

Determined that he would also be stuffed with information, the young Hubert built a tight-fitting wooden box to wear like a hat at all times, so changing the shape of his head as it grew, from a useless sphere to a fact-filled square. It is for this reason that he is now known within MP1 as "Cube". He is the organization's top brain box – literally. The rumour is that he still sleeps with his head in the frame to prevent it becoming spherical again. What I wouldn't give to see that square head right now.

The door to the lab whooshed open and Fangs entered. He was still clutching my Spookie award. "Thanks, boss," I said, reaching for it. "I'll find somewhere safe to put it."

"It's probably best if I keep hold of it for now," Fangs said. "It *is* a clue to Cube's disappearance, after all."

My hairy brow furrowed. "How is it a clue?" I asked.

"Well, Cube was giving it to me, er, I mean us, sorry, you, when the hotel was attacked. It may prove vital to solving this case."

"Forget about your trophy, Agent Enigma," bubbled a voice. We looked up to find Phlem slithering towards us. "It has nothing to do with the case, and everything else is on hold until we find Cube. We look after our own here at MP1."

"Of course, sir," I said.

Fangs tucked the award beneath his cape.

"Did you get the CCTV footage, Agent Brown?" Phlem asked.

"Right here, sir," I said, flipping open my laptop. A couple of key strokes later, and we were watching a black-and-white video of the outside of the Dorchester Hotel. "This is the moment when the suspects arrived..."

A lorry with a sign reading "Carpet Cleaners" on the side pulled up at the back of the hotel and eight identical skeletons climbed out.

There was a time when people might have been surprised or even scared to see something like that, but none of the few passers-by gave the bony bodies so much as a second glance. Ever since the supernatural equality laws had been passed, skeletons, vampires, witches and more were all accepted as part of society. The days of spooky characters only coming out at Halloween were long gone.

Some things hadn't changed, however. Just like in the human world, the supernatural one has its fair share of villains, and that's why Monster Protection, 1st Unit, was created – to track down and catch the world's worst criminal *monster*minds. There are agencies like MP1 operating across the globe. And now the bad guys

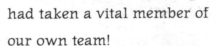

had taken a vital member of our own team!

Phlem was leaning in to peer at the screen. "I know them. It's the Bone Boys. Skeletal muscle for hire – if such a thing is possible."

"The action moves indoors now," I said, switching to a

different camera feed. The skeletons had gathered outside the doors to the ballroom. Each of them was holding a smoke bomb. Then one appeared to give a command and the skeletal crew stormed the room.

I brought up the footage from inside the ballroom. There wasn't much to see, though, as the room quickly filled up with smoke, totally obscuring the view.

"The only other shot I've got of them is this," I said, tapping in another command.

A video showed four of the skeletons scurrying out of the hotel carrying a white cage between them. There was something inside it, but it was hard to make out exactly what.

Phlem clicked "Pause" with a gloopy finger, leaving a few tendrils of slime on my keyboard. "I think we can all guess what's inside that cage..."

"We can, indeed," said Fangs. Then he added, "You mean Cube, don't you?"

"Yes, Agent Enigma," Phlem said. "I mean Cube."

"Where did they get the cage from?" I asked. "And where are the other four Bone Boys?"

"Take a closer look," said Phlem. "The other four skeletons *are* the cage. The Bone Boys have the ability to disassemble themselves to build just about anything they need: cages, weapons, vehicles. And because they're skeletons, they don't leave fingerprints behind."

I sighed. Working in the supernatural world was incredibly exciting, but it did have its challenges – skeletons didn't leave fingerprints, you couldn't photograph vampires, and werewolves only ever looked like their police mug shots once a month at full moon. Well, almost all werewolves.

I'm a bit different to my fellow lycanthropes. Something went wrong during my first transformation and I ended up permanently stuck as a hairy wolf. My school already had a couple of werewolves, but unless you were with them at full moon, you never saw them with their fur and claws. I'm the exact opposite. The full moon is the one night a month when I change back into a human. It hadn't exactly made my life easy.

My parents did their best to help. My dad even glued my stray hairs to his face and hands, so that I would look more like "one of the family" when we

went on days out. It didn't work – the stuck-on fur made him look more like a homeless yeti than a werewolf. Life at home was hard, and I wasn't very happy at all.

That all changed when I was recruited by MP1 and teamed up with Fangs Enigma – the world's greatest vampire spy (at least, that's what he calls himself). Since then, life has been a whirlwind of weapons-training, computer-hacking and secret assignments.

Phlem's voice dragged me back to the case at hand. "What did you find out from interviewing the hotel staff?" he asked Fangs.

"Well," said Fangs, "they all agreed that I totally deserved to win the Spookie Spy of the Year Award."

"What did the hotel staff say about *the Bone Boys*, Enigma?" Phlem said.

Fangs shrugged. "Not a lot, really. They had the right paperwork to clean the carpets – not that they did that. The duty manager just let them inside and told them to get on with it."

"Then we're back to square one," said Phlem with a sigh. It sounded like someone scuba-diving in a vat of gravy.

"Square one," I repeated, absent-mindedly. "Cube's favourite place to be."

Phlem clamped a slimy hand on my shoulder.
"Chin up, Agent Brown. We'll stop at nothing to
find Cube. He'll be back here before you know it."

"I don't see how," said Fangs. "We've got no
leads, no witnesses. In short, no way of tracing
Cube at all."

"That's where you're wrong, Agent Enigma,"
said Phlem. "We do have one way of tracing Cube,
even if it is a little unconventional by normal
standards." He tapped one of his front teeth with
his rubbery tongue, lighting it up blue. MP1 agents
communicate by a radio transmitter attached to
their front teeth. It can send and receive messages
instantly.

"Send him in," Phlem ordered.

The door to the lab slid open and another
vampire entered.

"Oh no..." groaned Fangs.

"Oh yes!" exclaimed the newcomer. "The
Astounding Claret is on the case."

The Astounding Claret was dressed in a
gold-sequined suit, purple silk vampire cape and
designer sunglasses. His slicked-back hair was
silvery-grey and his fangs sparkled like diamonds.

The glittery figure danced across the floor
to me. He took my paw in his hand and gently
kissed it.

"Enchanted to meet you, my dear," he crooned,
whipping off his rose-tinted glasses.

Then I saw his eyes for the first time, and I almost jumped with surprise. I'd seen those eyes before! Slowly, I turned to stare at my boss. He didn't look happy.

"Puppy Brown," he sighed. "Meet Claret Enigma – my dad."

Fangs pulled the key Phlem had given him from his pocket and let us into Cube's private apartment on the top floor of the MP1 Headquarters. Claret had claimed there would be something up here that would help him to locate Cube.

"I was an MP1 secret agent
for many years," Claret told
me as we made our way to
Cube's kitchen. "Your boss
was just a boy back then; he
still had his baby fangs. I was
really proud when he followed in
his old man's footsteps and trained to be a spy."

"So what made you leave the business?" I asked.

"I took early retirement," Claret replied.
"There's only so long a handsome vampire can
travel the world, catching bad guys and wooing
beautiful ladies."

I smiled. Claret reminded me so much of
my boss.

"Being a spy was even tougher in my day,"
Claret said. "No supernatural equality laws back
then, you see. Plain, vanilla humans didn't like
the idea of sharing their world with vamps and
wolves, so we had disguise chips embedded

30

beneath our skin to hide our true identities. Cube invented those."

"Did you know him well?" I asked.

Claret nodded. "Cube and I are old friends. We went to school together. In fact, I knew him back when the corners of his head were still rounded. We joined MPI at the same time. He went to work in the technical division, and I set out to rid the world of monstrous miscreants."

"Does Cube still have one of those old disguise chips beneath his skin?" I asked. "We could use it to track him down."

"No such luck," said Claret. "Only agents in the field got those babies. Besides, we won't need any of that old technology. Not with my unique talents."

"You still haven't said what your talents are," I pointed out. Phlem had slithered off shortly after Claret had arrived, saying the new vampire would explain everything.

"That's because he hasn't got any," said Fangs.

Claret arched a well-plucked eyebrow. "You know, son, you'd do well to open your mind a little. There are more things in this world than can be easily explained."

"There are more things in this kitchen than can be easily explained," said Fangs. "That suit, for example."

"Clients *do* expect a certain amount of razzle-dazzle in my line of work."

"What line of work is that?" I asked.

"My dad retired from MPI to set himself up as a private investigator," said Fangs. "A *psychic* private investigator."

"The Astounding Claret!" the older vampire announced with a smile. "I use my gifts to track down missing people, find lost pets and recover hidden fortunes – whatever my client requires, so long as it's legal, of course."

I was still none the wiser. "Your *gifts*?"

"I have what you laypersons often call 'second sight'," said Claret. "All the Astounding Claret has to do is touch something which has been in contact with the missing person and he can follow their energy line right to them. Works for missing belongings too."

"That's amazing."

"That's rubbish," scoffed Fangs. "And even if it was possible, it's no substitute for good, solid secret-agent work."

Claret smiled. "Fangs isn't exactly a fan of my new career," he said. "Nor does he believe that I can use astral-projection to travel outside my own body to possess another living creature's."

I could feel my eyes getting wider with every new claim. "And can you?"

"Of course he can't," snapped Fangs.

"I certainly can," Claret retorted. "It takes up a lot of energy but, if I concentrate hard enough, I can inhabit the body of any living thing."

He gave me a wink. "You wouldn't believe the number of missing pets I've found that way."

"How did you learn to do it?" I asked.

"I didn't," Claret replied. "It all happened by accident, years ago. Fangs had a pet rat when he was a kid. Stoker, it was called. It escaped one day while he was at school, and I knew I'd have to find it before he got home or he'd end up in tears."

"Tears?" Fangs muttered. "As if."

Claret winked at me again. "So, there I am, crawling around on the floor looking for this rat when, suddenly, I've got whiskers and I'm staring up at myself. I thought I must have banged my head at first – but it turned out I'd left my own body and possessed Stoker's!"

Fangs opened Cube's fridge and poured himself a glass of milk. "Then why have you come here? Can't you just possess a pigeon and fly off to find Cube?"

"Anyway, when Cube disappeared,

34

Phlem called me," said Claret, ignoring Fangs's last remark. "He never wanted me to retire and set up on my own. He said my skills could prove useful in certain MPI cases, so I promised to help out whenever I could."

He turned to look around the worktops. "Now, I just need something that Cube has touched recently – aha!" He snatched up a spray bottle filled with pink liquid. "'Heat-resistant cooking spray,'" he said, reading the handwritten label on its side.

Fangs almost choked on his milk. "That's ridiculous!"

"It does sound like one of Cube's inventions, though," I said.

Claret slumped back into a chair, his chest heaving and his eyelids fluttering.

Fangs watched his dad with a blank expression.

Then Claret sat bolt upright again and pointed straight ahead. "I have it!" he cried. "The Astounding Claret can see Cube's energy line."

"What does it look like?" I asked.

"Long and yellow," replied Claret. "But he's far away. His energy line is wearing very thin."

"It's not the only thing wearing thin," said Fangs.

"The Astounding Claret needs a plane," said Claret, jumping up. "I'll go and arrange one with Phlem." He raced out of the kitchen, his shiny purple cape wafting out behind him as he ran.

Thirty minutes later we were climbing through the clouds in the MPl private jet. Claret was at the controls so he could "follow" Cube's energy line. Fangs and I were in the cabin, talking to Phlem via a video link on my laptop.

"Agents Brown and Enigma," he rasped. "Anything to report?"

"The flight's not bad," said Fangs, "but I don't think much of the pilot."

"I don't care what you think," Phlem said. "I'm

pulling out all the stops to find Professor Cubit."

"It's your call," said Fangs. "But, in the meantime, there's a village somewhere that's badly missing its idiot."

Phlem ignored the sarcastic comment. "Agent Brown, you will find a flight case beneath your seat containing your gadgets for this assignment."

I slid the case out and put it on the table.

"How can we have gadgets if the man who makes them has been kidnapped?" asked Fangs.

"These are the inventions Cube most recently logged into the MP1 stores," Phlem explained. "We're reasonably certain he's worked out any glitches."

Fangs sighed.

I opened the case and then jumped back in surprise as something flew up into the air and began to whizz around the cabin.

"This is what Cube calls the Bat 'n' Ball," said Phlem.

I studied the gadget. It was a tennis ball with a pair of bat's wings stuck onto it. "How do we control it?" I asked.

"I'm uploading the relevant software to your laptop and Smartphone as we speak," said Phlem.

Next, I took a bar of soap from the case. "What's this?" I asked.

"According to Cube's paperwork, it's known as Sticky Soap," Phlem replied.

"I don't even want to ask..." said Fangs.

"You don't need to," said Phlem. "It does exactly what the name says. It's soap mixed with powerful glue. One wash and you're stuck."

"I'm sure we'll find a way to make use of it," I said.

"And the last one?" Fangs asked, peering into the now empty case. "The madness usually comes in threes..."

"Actually, you're already wearing the final

gadget, Agent Enigma," said Phlem with a hint of a smile. "You have been since you collected your dry-cleaning from the MP1 laundry."

Fangs stood and looked down at himself. "What?"

"Cube calls it Seat of Your Pants," Phlem went on. "There are chair legs built into the fabric of your trousers. To activate them, just put your hands in your back pocket and press the button."

Cautiously, Fangs moved into the cabin aisle and then followed Phlem's instructions. Four poles slid out from my boss's trousers – two from the trouser legs and two from the waistband – to form the legs of a chair.

Fangs sat back. "This is actually quite comfortable," he said. "It will come in really useful if I need a sit-down in the middle of a busy assignment. Cube's finally designed something that wor—"

There was a flash and a spark. Then the front chair legs expanded and catapulted my boss along the length of the cabin and through the curtain which separated us from the cockpit. Fangs landed on his dad's lap.

CRASH!

"This *is* turning into an exciting day!" Claret smiled. "First the Astounding Claret finds Cube's energy line – and now he gets an unexpected cuddle from his son."

"I'm not cuddling you," Fangs protested, working the button in his back pocket to try to retract the chair legs.

"Well, you should be," said Claret. "The Astounding Claret has figured out exactly where Cube's energy line ends. We're going to the Greek island of Rhodes."

The telescopic chair legs shrank back – but not quite all the way, forcing Fangs to walk out of the cockpit as though he was wearing a pair of stilts.

"I'm not going anywhere until I've had another drink," he mumbled.

I called the traffic control tower at Rhodes airport to give them our secret MPl password, "zombie brains". We were given permission to land at the far side of the airfield. Claret taxied the jet into a hangar that had been specially reserved for us.

We disembarked quickly, although Fangs
stepped cautiously down the stairs, like he
was walking over hot coals.

"Are you OK, boss?" I asked.

"Of course I'm not OK," he replied.
"I'm scared Cube's stupid chair
trousers might launch me into orbit
again. I'm never getting my dry-
cleaning done at MPI again, Puppy. I
might find scorpion stings embedded
in my bow tie next time."

We made our way to the main terminal,
where we mingled with holidaymakers and locals
alike. I noticed a black cat lurking behind us and
stopped to tickle it under the chin. The cat purred
and rubbed up against my legs.

"Where next?" I asked, standing up.

"I'm not sure," Claret replied. "Cube's energy
line is diffusing, making it difficult for the
Astounding Claret to follow it further."

"Of course it is," said Fangs. "Whenever he's called upon to give specific information, the Astounding Claret loses the trail."

"Then what do *you* propose we do?" Claret demanded.

"We do it the old-fashioned way," said Fangs. "We interrogate the locals." He spun round and grabbed the black cat, then held it at arm's length. "I know a witch's cat when I see one," he snarled. "Why have you been following us?"

The cat hissed, then he karate-chopped Fangs on the neck, kicked him in the stomach and flipped him onto his back. He ran up Fangs's chest and glared down into his face. "My name is Feline Scamper. I'm a local secret agent based here in Rhodes and attached to Monster Protection, 2nd Unit."

"That's the mainland Europe division," I said, helping my boss to his feet

44

as the cat leapt to the floor. "We didn't call ahead for local assistance."

"I was already at the airport, tracking someone," said Feline. "Then I heard the password 'zombie brains' had been used, and I thought I'd better check out what my fellow agents were up to."

"Who are you tracking?" asked Claret.

"Someone who is here to collect a delivery," said Feline. "The tenth this week. All identical wooden crates, all flying in from Syria. They pass through the security scanners without a problem, but something about them feels wrong to me."

"Now that's a real spy talking," said Fangs with a grin. "Working off clues and hunches. That's how we'll find Cube in the end. None of this psychic nonsense."

"Who's Cube?" asked Feline.

"Professor Hubert Cubit, the head of MPI's technical division," I replied. "He was snatched from London last night, and we believe he's been brought to Rhodes. That's why we're here."

"Well, *one* of us believes that," said Fangs with a glance at his dad.

"I'm telling you, his energy line ends here," said Claret.

"Perhaps we could help each other out," Feline suggested. "After all, we're both on Monster Protection cases on the same island. Maybe one of my fellow agents has some information about this missing friend of yours."

"That's a great idea," I said. "First, though, we'll try and help you. Tell us about these crates."

"They've all been sealed with a highly sophisticated numerical lock," Feline explained, "and we don't know the access code to look inside. The same person has collected all of the crates. We could arrest her, but we don't want to scare off the end buyer."

"Her?" said Fangs.

Feline smiled. "That's
her at the arrivals gate.
The one in the black
dress. Her name is
Marmalade Springs."

Fangs removed
his sunglasses and
studied the woman.
She had long, curly
black hair and
sparkling brown eyes.
"Getting the code should
be no problem." He slipped
his sunglasses back on.
"Give me five minutes."

"No!" cried Feline. "You'll
blow the whole operation."

But it was too late. My boss was already
hurrying towards the woman – and Claret was
right beside him. Feline and I dashed after them.

"Where do you think you're going?" Fangs demanded of Claret.

"To interrogate the suspect with you," said his dad.

"I don't need some old man to help me talk to a beautiful woman."

"I think you'll find that this old man still has a few tricks up his sleeve," said Claret.

The two vampires were so lost in their argument that they collided with Marmalade Springs, sending her crashing to the ground. She cried out in surprise.

Fangs took Marmalade's hand to help her to her feet.

"I'm so sorry, miss," he said. "We didn't see you."

Marmalade snatched her hand away, only for Claret to grab it.

"What my insolent son means to say is that *he*

48

didn't *see* you," the older vampire soothed. "I was simply dazzled by your incredible beauty."

But Marmalade pulled her hand away from Claret too. She looked around, nervously. "Go away!" she said, snatching up her purse. "I'm meeting someone."

"Who?" said Fangs.

"Nobody!" Marmalade hissed. Then she hurried away.

"Thanks for that!" Feline scowled. "I've been following Miss Springs all week hoping to find out what she's been collecting and for whom, and now all that work is ruined."

"Oh, I wouldn't say that," said Claret with a wink. "I think this must have dropped out of her purse when she fell over." He held up a piece of paper on which was scribbled a six-digit number. "I think it's her phone number."

"Or it could be the code for the locks on those crates," suggested Feline.

"The code," said Claret. "Yes, of course. I used my skills as a pick-pocket to retrieve the secret code."

"You did nothing of the sort," scoffed Fangs. "Her purse was wide open, and the piece of paper was sticking out. I could have taken it myself."

"No need to be jealous that you didn't, son," said Claret. "Now where are these crates?"

Feline led us through airport security and into a warehouse filled with the bags and boxes that had been unloaded from that day's various inbound flights.

"There it is," said Feline, gesturing at a large wooden crate in the corner of the shed. There was an air vent in the top and a computer keypad fixed to the front. "It's exactly the same as the last nine."

"Except you'll get to find out what's inside this one," Claret said. "All thanks to the Astounding Claret." He took a step towards the keypad.

Fangs snatched the sheet of paper from his dad's

hand. "You've done your bit for today. Leave this to a real vampire spy..." He tapped the code – 180910 – into the numerical lock. There was a *CLICK!*, and a *WHIRR!*, and the front panel of the crate dropped open to reveal – hamsters!

Thousands and thousands of *hamsters...*

A great furry tidal wave descended upon us, sweeping us off our feet and carrying us into the middle of the cargo shed.

SQUEAK!

I don't have the words to describe the sound of several thousand hamsters, all squeaking at the same time. The crate must have been sound-proofed as we'd heard nothing before Fangs had opened it.

Fangs! I'd lost sight of my boss in the sudden chaos. I gazed across the sea of hamsters. A hand was pushing up through the furry mass, a hand that was clutching my Spookie award. I couldn't

believe he'd actually
brought it with him.

"Forget me," Fangs croaked. "Just save the
award!"

I forced my way through the animals, taking as
much care as I could not to stand on any of them,

and grabbed Fangs's hand. Claret also clamped a hand around my boss's wrist to help me pull him out.

Fangs's head broke the surface of the hamsters. A small, beige hamster was trying to burrow into his ear. I pulled it out and sent it scurrying on its away.

Claret hugged his son. "I thought I'd lost you," he cried. "And I didn't want to have to explain that you'd met your end at the tiny paws of a few hamsters."

"A *few* hamsters?" spat Fangs. "There are thousands of the things!"

The whole warehouse suddenly started shaking. No, not just the warehouse, but the ground as well. I grabbed a trolley and hung onto it as bags and boxes tumbled off their piles and onto the ground around us.

"It's an earthquake!" I cried, as everything

around us started to move very, very fast. One second I was clinging onto the luggage trolley, and the next, I was on the other side of the warehouse, holding Fangs's hand, and talking incredibly quickly. Claret and Feline had also moved in the blink of an eye.

Then as suddenly as it had sped up, the world slowed down again.

"Now that," I said, "was weird."

From the outside, the MP2 Headquarters looked like an ordinary holiday villa in the hills, but, inside, was a brightly lit and air-conditioned corridor that led deep into the mountainside. Feline showed us into a modern laboratory staffed entirely by witches. One of them cackled as she limped across the room to us.

"So these are the agents from MP1?" she said.

"They look delicious, especially this one." She sidled up to Fangs and squeezed his arm like she was testing the freshness of a loaf of bread.

Fangs didn't react. I think he was still stunned from being smothered by hamsters.

"That'll do, Kora," said Feline. "I've brought these people here to help them, not cook them. She's a brilliant geologist," the cat whispered to me as the witch hobbled away, "but she just can't leave her old Gingerbread House days behind."

Once the earthquake had ended, Feline had called in a team of witches' cats to shepherd the hamsters back into their crate – but it had still taken over an hour. Fangs had spent most of that time sitting silently on an upturned suitcase, clutching the Spookie award.

Kora launched a complex piece of software on her computer. "The earthquake registered five point nine on the Richter scale," she said, indicating a graph filled with jagged lines. "Except it wasn't really an earthquake."

"Of course it was," said Claret. "The earth was quaking. We felt it."

Kora shook her head. Her lank, green hair slapped against her cheeks. "It's only an earthquake if there is an epicentre – a point where the disturbance starts. Whatever this was, it happened all over the world at exactly the same time."

She launched a page of news clippings. An "earthquake" had been reported in London, Rio, Sydney, New York and Beijing. It had happened everywhere at once.

"If it wasn't an earthquake, what was it?" I asked.

Kora cackled with delight again. "The world sped up!"

I stared at her in astonishment. *"What?"*

The witch tapped at a spike in the graph with a cracked fingernail. "The rotation of the earth increased in speed for ninety seconds."

"But ... that's impossible."

Kora screamed with laughter at my disbelief and danced on the spot.

Feline studied the data on the screen. "She's right," he said. "At the equator, the earth spins at one thousand six hundred and fifty kilometres per hour. However, for a minute and a half this morning, the planet rotated at almost two thousand kilometres per hour."

I still couldn't get my head around it. "But how?"

"Your guess is as good as mine," said Feline. "Any theories, Kora?" The witch wasn't listening. She was still dancing a jig, her ragged skirt hitched up in her hands.

Suddenly, Fangs screamed. "The hamster's back," he cried, pointing to a tiny rodent scampering towards us. "That one tried to burrow into my brain!"

He made to run, but Feline leapt into his path. "That is not a hamster," he hissed. "It is a mouse – and a highly valued MP2 agent as well."

"You mean he's not going to try to get inside my skull?"

"Not unless you annoy him," said Feline. "This is Stavros Feta. He followed Miss Springs from the airport earlier."

The mouse clambered up the leg of the desk to sit in front of Feline, whiskers twitching. "I saw everythin', innit," he squeaked.

"So, where did she go?"

"To Lindos, guvnor," said Stavros. "To the Acropolis."

Feline brought up a map of Rhodes on the computer. Lindos was a town in the south-east of the island. "The Acropolis is what is left of the Temple of Athena," he explained, showing us a photograph. "It's over two thousand three hundred years old."

Claret gasped. "That's it! The Astounding Claret can see Cube's energy line again, and it leads there."

"What's at the Acropolis now?" I asked.

"Nothing," said Feline. "It's a tourist attraction, and a place for couples to get married. Nothing sinister at all."

"That's what you think, squire," said Stavros. "Just you wait till you hear who Miss Springs met up there – the one she's been ordering them crates of hamsters for."

"Why?" asked Feline. "Who is it?"

Stavros paused dramatically.

"Nobody."

Fangs blinked.

"She's been delivering these crates to nobody?"

"That's right," said the mouse. "*Mr* Nobody."

His words had quite an effect. Feline Scamper recoiled. Kora stopped dancing and her face became pale green. The other witches in the laboratory froze, and one of them dropped a test tube that smashed on the stone floor.

"No!" said Feline. "That's impossible. He's dead."

"Who's dead?" asked Fangs. "Who's Mr Nobody?"

"Follow me," said the cat. "I'll show you." He led the way to his office.

I say "office" – it was more like the cat section of a pet shop. Feline curled up in a foam bed and lapped at a bowl of milk, while Claret, Fangs and I sat awkwardly on various scratching posts.

"I don't suppose you have any more milk, do you?" Fangs asked.

Feline shook his head. "Sorry," he said. "This is the last of it, although you're welcome to share..."

For a moment, I actually thought Fangs was going to kneel down beside the cat and start lapping at the white liquid in the bowl – but instead, he just crossed his legs and shook his head.

Meanwhile, Stavros had scurried over to a computer and entered his password to gain access to the MP2 network. It looked like he was tap dancing on the keyboard. He brought up the file for our suspect.

"Mr Nobody was a right nasty piece of work, innit?" the mouse squeaked. "Extortion, money laundering, organized crime – you name it, this geezer had a hand in it."

"So, why would he need the hamsters?" I asked. "Some sort of experiment?"

"Maybe," Stavros said. "But he's a criminal, not a scientist. He brings doctors, scientists, and what-not in to work for him whenever he needs 'em.

Whether they like it or not."

"That would explain why he might have kidnapped Cube," Claret said.

"But you said Nobody was dead," I reminded Feline. "What happened? How did he die?"

"He said it was going to be his biggest job," Feline explained. "The one the criminal world would remember him for. He was going to be famous. Infamous. Stavros was our man on the inside..."

"S'right, guvnor," said the mouse, taking up the story. "Took months of me runnin' errands and sortin' out little problems for Mr Nobody to finally trust me."

Claret's brow furrowed. "What kind of 'little problems'?" he asked.

The mouse shrugged – which was something I never thought I'd see.

"The usual stuff," he said. "If someone didn't pay protection money, I'd sneak in and nibble through the electrical wiring in their shop or business. By the time the fire brigade arrived, there'd be nothin' left to protect, if you catch my meanin'. The verdict was always fire caused by poor electrical maintenance."

"You burned down people's businesses?!" I exclaimed. "That's awful!"

"I had to appear legit, didn't I, sweetheart?" said Stavros. "I had to make Mr Nobody think I was someone he could rely on. And MP2 always reimbursed the victims for their losses, on the quiet like."

"You still haven't told us how this guy died," Fangs pointed out.

"I'm gettin' to that bit, ain't I?" Stavros squeaked. "Like the boss said, it was gonna be Mr Nobody's biggest heist. A bank job worth sixty million Euros."

"That's a lot of money," said Claret with a whistle. "Did the police get him?"

"Nothing so simple, I'm afraid," said Feline.

"As Stavros had tipped us off about the robbery, MP2 were on hand to apprehend the villains – but we had to let them get into the vault and steal the money first so we had something to charge Mr Nobody with. He had a team of very expensive, very clever lawyers who could get him off just about everything."

"So what went wrong?" I asked.

"No one knows, darlin'," said Stavros. "Mr Nobody cracked the software that controlled the door to the bank's vault. It was halfway open when it suddenly started to shut again. Mr Nobody was trapped in the middle and the door squeezed him stone dead."

"That's horrible," I said.

"It wasn't pretty, right enough."

"Could he have faked his own death?" asked Claret.

Stavros shook his tiny head. "Nah, I saw the lot. It was real, all right."

"But you said Marmalade delivered the crate of hamsters to him today," said Fangs. "If he's dead, how is that possible?"

Stavros fixed my boss with a hard, mousey stare. "Because he's come back, guv," he said. "Mr Nobody has come back as a *ghost*."

Fangs pulled a bottle of black pills from his pocket and popped one into his mouth. Cube had invented these for him. They contained the "essence of midnight", and allowed a vampire to go out in the sun. My boss certainly needed them today. It was pushing 40 degrees Celsius. Not exactly the ideal weather for someone covered from head to toe in fur, either!

Fangs offered his dad one of the pills.

"I haven't had one of these in years," said Claret. "The Astounding Claret usually meets his clients at night."

"Well, the dark does provide a certain amount of anonymity for those who might be embarrassed about booking your services," said Fangs.

Feline had stayed at MP2, but had arranged for a car to drive us the few miles from Headquarters to Lindos – a picturesque tourist village where every building was painted a brilliant white. Above us on a hill towered the ancient ruins of the Acropolis.

"Cube is up there somewhere," said Claret, pointing up at the monument. "The Astounding Claret can see his energy line as clear as day."

"Then that's where we're going," I said. "According to Feline, it's quite a steep walk up to the Acropolis. Holidaymakers rent donkeys to make the journey."

Fangs looked at me as though I'd gone insane. "A donkey?" he cried. "You won't catch me on one of those things. I'd lose my cool."

We walked through narrow streets, lined with cafes, restaurants and gift shops. The Greek Islands had been among the signatories to the supernatural equality laws, and so the crowds of tourists included trolls, gremlins and ogres as well as ordinary humans. I even spotted a Minotaur enjoying a beer in one of the bars we passed.

I launched a GPS app on my phone to get my bearings. "We need to follow this street to the end, then turn right to head up the trail to the Acropolis, boss," I said. There was no reply. "Boss?"

I looked up to find Fangs staring over a low wall to our left, his gaze fixed on the beach below. "Well, well ... who do we have here?" he mused aloud.

When Claret and I joined him, I immediately saw what he was looking at. Marmalade Springs was kneeling in the sand, digging a hole with a small, plastic spade.

"Miss Springs could be our way inside the Acropolis," said Fangs, leaping over the wall and striding across the beach towards her.

"We'd better go with him," said Claret. "He didn't make the best first impression with her this morning."

I was about to point out that Claret hadn't exactly hit it off with her either, but he had already jumped over the wall and was now running after Fangs, his purple cape flapping out behind him. I followed as quickly as I could.

It was fair to say that Marmalade Springs didn't look pleased to see us. After all, here were the two vampires who had knocked her off her feet at the airport – and they were about to accost her on the beach. She froze – if such a thing were possible in this heat.

"What do you lot want?" she demanded.

"To get to the bottom of something," said Fangs. "This morning, when I asked who you were meeting, you said nobody. You meant 'Nobody' with a capital 'N'. *Mr* Nobody, to be precise."

Marmalade's terrified eyes darted around the beach. "I don't know what you're talking about."

"I think you do," I said. "And I'm asking for your help. We have to speak to Mr Nobody; we believe he knows where our friend is."

"I don't know anyone by that name."

"OK," said Fangs. "Let's start at the beginning. Why are you here, building sandcastles?"

"I'm not building sandcastles," said Marmalade. "I'm digging up pebbles." She gestured to a red bucket beside her. It was filled to the brim with smooth stones.

"OK," said Claret. "What are you collecting pebbles for?"

"A scientist needs them," said Marmalade quietly.

"A scientist?" I asked. "What's his name?"

"I don't know," Marmalade admitted. "I'm sorry about your friend, but I really shouldn't be talking to you..." She turned to leave, but Fangs grabbed her arm.

"This scientist," he said, "what shape is his head?"

"It's square – which is very odd. Now, I've told you enough. I have to go..."

73

"Cube!" exclaimed Claret. "It has to be. I told you he was here."

"Can you get us inside the Acropolis?" I asked.

Before Marmalade could reply, the sand around her began to shift, and there was a sound I'd heard before...

CLICK! SNAP! CRACK! SNICK!

"Oh no!" she cried. "They're here!"

Suddenly two skeletons rose up from beneath the sand. Marmalade screamed and ran out into the sea. The two skeletons pulled something large and white from the hole they'd created. It was a raft built out of shining white bones – presumably taken from one or more of their colleagues.

Marmalade tried to swim away, but the skeletons were too fast. They pushed Marmalade onto the raft and kicked their fleshless legs against the tide, heading further out to sea.

Claret, Fangs and I plunged into the surf to

swim after her when two more of the Bone Boys
rose up out of the water in front of us.

"Get out of our way!" Fangs yelled.

But the skeletons didn't move. Instead, they
each ripped off an arm bone and began
to beat my boss with them like clubs.

"Ow! Ow! OW!" yelled Fangs.
"That really hurts."

"I'll take that, thank you,"
cried Claret. He snatched
the bone from the
nearest attacker and
hurled it out to sea.
The skeleton lunged
at him, wrapping its thin
fingers around his throat and
pushing him beneath the
waves. I was about to help when
the second skeleton turned and
pounced on me.

75

My vision blurred as I was forced beneath the water. The skeleton wasn't strong, but he did have an advantage in that he didn't need to breathe. All he had to do was keep me under the surface for long enough and the sea would do the rest of the work for him.

The water churned beside me as Claret wrestled with the other skeleton. Fangs was trying to help him while still holding our Spookie award out of the water. He swung it back, and hit the skeleton on the head with the trophy, knocking his skull clean off.

The assassin went limp and fell back to bob gently
on the surface of the sea.

So the Bone Boys had a weakness after all!
Knock their heads off and they couldn't
fight any more. The knowledge
gave me hope and
a burst of
energy.

I forced myself up to the surface and sucked in a long lungful of air. "You know," I said, glaring at my attacker. "You really shouldn't wave a bone about in front of a little doggie like me." Then I opened my jaws and clamped my teeth around the skeleton's neck bone. I shook the bad guy from side to side until, with a satisfying **CLICK!**, his skull fell off.

A scream pierced the air, and I turned to see the two skeletons dragging Marmalade out of the water and up the beach. The two became three as the Bone Boy who had formed the raft put himself back together again. I had a feeling it wouldn't be long before the two skeletons in the water with us found and reattached their skulls. We had to move fast.

"Let's get after her!" cried Fangs.

"What if these guys come after us?" Claret asked.

Fangs snatched a skull that happened to be floating past. He wedged it tightly inside the ribcage of the nearest Bone Boy. "They haven't got the *guts*," he snarled.

We ran for the path that led up to the Acropolis, dodging between tourists, and were just in time to see the bad guys put Marmalade onto the back of a donkey that was manned by the final Bone Boy. The animal took off at top speed as the other skeletons disappeared into the crowd.

Fangs, Claret and I jumped on long-eared

steeds of our own – although my boss didn't
look very happy about it. Still, we had to save
Marmalade. We couldn't allow her to be hurt for
talking to us.

Most tourists take the winding, cobbled streets
up to the Acropolis at a slow, leisurely pace so they
can enjoy the sights and take photographs of the
stunning views. But we didn't have that luxury.
Digging our heels into the donkeys' sides, we
galloped up the street, shouting at holidaymakers
to get out of the way.

Our donkeys, used to more sedate movement,
appeared to relish the chance to finally let loose,
and they ran faster and faster, their hooves
clattering against the cobbles. I've travelled in a
lot of unusual ways since joining MP1, but this
had to be the strangest.

Before long, we caught sight of Marmalade
and her donkey ahead of us. Claret pulled on
his reins, urging his donkey on.

Fangs was lagging behind, though. His donkey was wheezing hard, its nostrils flared. After one final loud bray, it sank to the ground, exhausted.

"Get up!" shouted Fangs, pulling the reins – but it was no good. His ride was over. Cursing, he leapt off the back of the beast and ran after Claret and me.

Our donkeys ran on, scattering a wedding party on their way up to the chapel near the top of the hill. Guests screamed as we charged through them. A woman I took to be the mother of the groom gave Claret a clout on the back of the head with her handbag.

Marmalade's donkey had reached the top of the hill. Her skeletal kidnapper pulled her towards a set of ancient stone pillars at the far end of the ruins. Claret and I jumped off our own donkeys and gave chase.

The skeleton reached the first pillar and slid the bone of its index finger into a metal sphere drilled into the stone. A hidden doorway opened in the rock and the bad guy pushed Marmalade inside.

I'd seen that type of lock before; they're called isomorphic, and they're impossible to crack. The lock will only open when activated by registered DNA – something skeletons do have. If your genetic code isn't listed in the computer database, the lock simply won't open for you.

The door was already sliding shut. We weren't going to make it – unless...

I pulled a screwdriver from my utility belt and threw it. It clattered to the ground, rolled and wedged in the gap, stopping the door from closing by just a few centimetres.

"Good shot!" said Claret.

"Thanks," I said, hooking my claws around the stone portal and beginning to pull. Even with Claret helping me,

83

forcing the door back open by hand was difficult, and it was a few minutes before we had created a space large enough to squeeze through. We couldn't see anything in the darkness beyond.

Fangs staggered up to us. His normally crisp, white shirt was slick with sweat.

"What kept you?" asked Claret.

"The world's only asthmatic donkey," Fangs replied. "Still, it was a *wheeze*."

I noticed that he had lipstick marks all over his cheeks. "Are you sure the donkey was the only reason you fell behind?"

Fangs winked.

"Someone had to apologize to the bridesmaids you almost ran over." He smiled. "Now where's Marmalade?"

"Somewhere down there," I said.

"Then let's go," said Fangs.

We stepped into the tunnel and let the door slam shut behind us. I pulled the torch from my utility belt and switched it on.

"Cube's energy line is here," said Claret, "but it's very faint. The poor fellow must be exhausted."

"He's not the only one," said Fangs. "I had to run up at least half of that hill."

"Well, we're heading back down now," I pointed out as the tunnel twisted to the left and spiralled downwards.

Eventually, we reached another door. This one, thankfully, only had a standard lock. "We must be right underneath the Acropolis," I whispered as I picked the lock with one of my claws.

"Not a bad place for a hideout," said Fangs.

As soon as the lock clicked, Claret pressed his hand against the door and made to push it open. Fangs grabbed his wrist to stop him.

"What are you doing?" he hissed.

"Going to find Cube," said Claret. "His energy line leads right inside."

"You're getting slack in your old age," said Fangs. "There could be anything waiting for us behind that door."

"Like what?"

Fangs rolled his eyes. "At the very best, a legion of Nobody's skeletons will be waiting to strip us of our flesh and dance around in our skin."

Claret considered the suggestion. "So what do we do?"

"Well, why don't you finally prove you can do this astral-projection thing you've been boasting about and find a spider to possess for a look around?"

"I'm not sure that would work," said Claret, looking uncomfortable. "I've never tried it underground before, you see. I don't know if I'd be able to achieve the necessary level of

cosmic karma. It's probably best if we think
of another way."

"Not to worry," I said quickly to avoid an
argument. "We've got everything we need for
reconnaissance right here."

"We have?" said Fangs.

I nodded. "Can I borrow your sunglasses for
a minute?"

Fangs slid his precious sunglasses off and
handed them over. I snapped them in half.

"What are you doing?" my boss cried.

"I need the camera," I explained, carefully
fishing out the tiny lens.

"And you couldn't get it without breaking my
glasses?" Fangs's voice echoed back along the
stone corridor.

"Ssh," said Claret.

"Don't you shush me, old man," Fangs spat.
"This is your fault. You owe me a new pair of
sunglasses."

"You can have mine, if you like," said Claret, offering his rose-tinted pair.

"They'll do for now," said Fangs. "But don't think this is over."

"Oh, I've no doubt about that," muttered Claret.

The two vampires glared at each other. Meanwhile, I pulled two of Cube's gadgets – the Bat 'n' Ball and the Sticky Soap – from my utility belt. I planned on using the soap to stick the camera from Fangs's sunglasses to the Bat 'n' Ball.

Once the camera was secure, I launched the Bat 'n' Ball control software on my Smartphone and then I popped the ball through the gap

between the door and the frame. It
flapped its bat's wings and soared up
into the air. Now we had a bird's
eye view of whatever was beyond
the tunnel. It was a vast underground cavern.

"Funny," said Claret. "I can't see an army of
skin-stealing skeletons."

Fangs gave a snarl. "What's that?" he asked,
pointing to a huge metallic pole spinning in the
centre of the room.

I swung the camera in for a closer look. "It's a
drill!" I exclaimed. "A drill as big as a skyscraper."
I angled the camera down to see where the drill
ended – and my jaw dropped open. There, cut
into the floor of the cavern, was
a hole the size of a lake. The
gigantic drill disappeared down
into it like a train vanishing into
a tunnel – if train tunnels were
ever vertical.

I flew the Bat 'n' Ball down into the hole.

"It goes down for miles!" said Fangs in amazement.

After emerging from the hole, the camera picked out someone moving through a door at the far side of the cavern. I instructed the ball to flap over for a closer look and almost cried with joy.

It was Cube!

We slipped through the door and made our
way around the outside of the cavern as quietly
as we could just in case there were any Bone
Boys hanging around. The huge drill bit was

even more impressive close up. It hung from a large motor built into the ceiling of the cave, and rotated, slowly but purposely, as it pushed down into the hole. Next to it, also hanging from the ceiling, were a dozen giant balls made from clear plastic.

I pulled out my Smartphone and took a couple of photographs of the drill and the balls. The pictures might be useful as evidence later.

We paused at the door on the other side of the cavern while Fangs ran his fingertips around the doorframe to check for booby traps. I activated the video camera function on my phone and held it up. By angling the screen, I was able to examine the layout of the room beyond. It was a laboratory filled with glass jars, Bunsen burners and many other items of high-tech scientific machinery. There was no one else in the room aside from Cube.

"It's all clear," whispered Fangs.

I burst into the laboratory and flung my arms

around Cube, hugging him tightly. "Professor!"
I cried.

"Puppy!" Cube hugged me back. "How did you
find me?"

"They called in an expert," said a voice from
the doorway.

Cube peered over the top of his glasses. "Is
that ... is that *Claret Enigma*?"

"It certainly is, my old friend," said Claret,
hurrying over to shake hands. "As soon as they
said you were missing, I came to help. And it
worked! I followed your energy line all the way
here."

"I helped as well," said Fangs, stepping between
Cube and his dad. "There's no substitute for good,
old-fashioned spy work."

"It doesn't matter who found him," I said,
grinning. "He's safe now."

"Thank you," exclaimed Cube. "Thank you all."

I threw my arms around the professor again.

I was delighted he was unharmed, although there was something different about him. His head was no longer square! Cube's skull was now the shape of a rugby ball.

"What have they done to you?" I asked.

"I rounded out the edges a little," said a voice.

We spun round to see four of the Bone Boys standing in the doorway behind us, each holding a hefty bone club. They seemed to be a little worse for wear after their encounter with us at the beach: one was missing an arm while another had a skull wedged inside his ribcage.

But it wasn't the skeletons who had spoken. I was confused until the air in front of us began to shimmer and a ghost materialized. Completely transparent, he wore a well-tailored suit, and had thick, slicked-back hair. He matched the photograph Feline had shown us at the MP2 Headquarters.

Mr Nobody.

"You can
tell your skinless
wonders to put their clubs away," said Fangs.
"They don't scare us."

"Actually, they scare me a bit," said Claret,
slowly raising his hands in the air. "I think it's
only fair to tell you that if you want to dance
around in my skin, you may need to find a belt;
my skin is getting a little saggy in my old age."

"Tell me what you've done to Cube!"
I demanded.

Mr Nobody smiled with his transparent lips. It wasn't a pretty sight. "The professor was less than keen to help me at first," he said. "So for every hour he withheld his co-operation, I rounded out the corners of his head a little."

"I could feel my intelligence seeping away," Cube groaned. "In the end, I had to do what he said, or I wouldn't have been able to think straight! But I don't know the whole plan. He didn't let me in on that."

"Why do you want Cube?" Fangs asked the ghost. "What's your plan?"

"I'd tell you *exactly* what I'm doing, Agent Enigma," he said. "But I think you'd find it more exciting if I *showed* you."

The skeleton guards handcuffed our hands behind our backs – using their own bones – then marched us out into the vast chamber. Mr Nobody walked ahead, his feet not quite making contact with the ground.

"You will have noticed my rather impressive drilling operation," he said. "Although, that is only stage one of my scheme. Allow me to show you stage two..."

He nodded to one of the skeletons, who opened a metal doorway I hadn't noticed before. There was a **HISS!** and clouds of icy air wafted out, temporarily obscuring our view of what was inside.

Then we saw it. Lying on a table made from ice was ... Mr Nobody – or, rather, Mr Nobody's body. It was dressed exactly the same as the ghost hovering beside us.

"It almost looks as though I'm asleep, doesn't it?" said the ghost of Mr Nobody, as he gazed lovingly down at his body. He attempted to stroke the hair of the corpse, but his spectral hand simply passed right through the head.

"You're not asleep, though, are you," said Fangs. "You're dead. Mr Nobody has no body."

I expected Mr Nobody to react angrily to Fangs's comment, but his left eye only twitched as he forced a smile. "For now," he said.

One of the skeletons closed the door to keep in the frozen air. Mr Nobody wafted away across the cavern again, and a nudge in the back from the skeletons told us we were meant to follow.

"I always expected to be killed one day," Mr Nobody told us. "When you work in crime, it's something of an occupational hazard. I did, however, assume I'd go out in a battle with the police rather than an unfortunate accident with a door to a bank vault."

"That must have been a *crushing blow*," quipped Fangs.

I saw Mr Nobody's eye twitch again, only

through the back of his see-through head this time, which looked very weird.

"I had a team of doctors on standby for such an occurrence," the ghost continued. "They repaired the damage to my internal organs and placed my body in its current cryogenically frozen state. Ready for when I return to it."

"But that's impossible," I cried. "You can't bring the dead back to life – not unless you come back as a zombie."

Mr Nobody spun in the air to face me. "Miss Brown," he snapped, "I have an IQ greater than Albert Einstein. When I come back, it will not be as a shuffling monster whose only thoughts are where to get a nice juicy brain for breakfast and whether my arms will stay attached to their sockets for the rest of the day."

"Puppy's right, Nobody," said Claret. "I've been involved with the spookier side of the supernatural world ever since I retired, and I know that once you've been separated from your body, there's no going back in there. The technology simply doesn't exist to bring someone back from the dead."

"You're correct, of course," said Mr Nobody. "Such technology doesn't *exist* – yet. And that's why I needed the help of Professor Cubit."

"Now I *know* you're insane," snapped Fangs. "Cube's good at what he does – and I never thought I'd have to say that in front of him – but even he can't build something that will bring you back from the dead."

Mr Nobody threw back his transparent head and laughed. "Oh, I know that," he said. "That sort of technology is centuries away."

"So what is it that you want Cube to do?" I asked.

Mr Nobody smiled. "I want him to help me speed up time."

No one spoke for a few seconds. We simply stared at Mr Nobody in amazement.

"How can you possibly speed up time?" I asked finally.

"Allow me to demonstrate," Mr Nobody replied. He turned to the nearest skeleton. "Get Marmalade."

A few seconds later, the guard returned with Marmalade Springs. "Which one of them was it?" Mr Nobody asked her.

Marmalade looked from Fangs to his dad and back again. "That one," she said, pointing at Claret. "They both knocked me to the ground, but it was the older one who took the code from me."

"Search him," Mr Nobody ordered his skeletons. Two rifled through Claret's pockets until they found the code for the box we'd opened at the airport. Meanwhile, three other Bone Boys wheeled in the crate of hamsters and a portable barbecue filled with searing hot coals.

Marmalade tapped the code into the keypad on the crate. She carefully lifted the lid and we could suddenly hear the thousands of hamsters squeaking inside. She chose one, then shut the crate again.

"Is the fluid ready?" Mr Nobody asked.

Cube nodded reluctantly. A skeleton scurried

into the lab and returned holding a spray bottle very similar to the one we had found in Cube's kitchen.

"I've improved the mixture," Cube said. "But I can't promise that it will last longer than the previous versions—"

"Take it," Mr Nobody told Marmalade, cutting Cube off. She snatched the bottle and sprayed the hamster in her hand with pink liquid. Then she tossed the hamster into the flames of the barbecue.

"No!" I cried. But I needn't have worried — because there, scuttling happily over the red hot coals, was a completely unharmed hamster.

Marmalade plucked it from the inferno with a pair of tongs and placed it on the ground. The creature looked around for a moment, then twitched its whiskers and ran off.

"Of course," I said, realization dawning. "Cube's heat-resistant cooking spray!"

"Well done, Miss Brown," said Mr Nobody. "And to think, I only know about it because Professor Cubit boasted about his discovery on an Internet cooking forum."

Cube's rounder-than-normal cheeks flushed red. "I didn't think there'd be a use for it at MPI, so I decided to share it with my fellow amateur chefs."

"It still doesn't make any sense," said Fangs. "Being able to heat hamsters doesn't give you the ability to speed up time."

"Oh, but it does, Agent Enigma," Mr Nobody said. He floated over to the giant drill. "I have now drilled further into the earth than anyone has ever done before. In fact – right to the earth's core."

Claret's eyes bulged. "But that's imp—"

Mr Nobody held up a hand to silence him. "If one more person claims what I am doing is impossible, I will explode!"

"Yeah, well, that'll be you *all over*," Fangs quipped. *"All over your lair."*

Another eye twitch, then the ghostly villain continued to rant. "I *have* drilled to the earth's core, and I *can* speed up time with hamsters!" He paused to take a deep breath and control his temper.

"You see, these are Syrian racing hamsters," said Mr Nobody, gesturing towards the crate. "Every one of them – in each of the ten shipments I have received – has been trained to run in one specific direction. The same direction in which the earth spins."

I glanced nervously at Fangs. I didn't like where this was going.

"I intend to drop a million heat-resistant hamsters into the earth's core," announced

Mr Nobody, his eyes twinkling with delight. "There, they will run as one, speeding up the rotation of the earth and therefore time itself. Months will pass in a matter of days, decades within a week – entire centuries will whizz by. Then, when science has invented a way to return my body back from the dead, I shall return the earth to its standard pace and rise once more from beyond the grave!"

There was a slight pause and then the skeletons began to applaud, their flesh-free hands clacking together like snooker balls.

CLICK! CLACK! CRACK!

"It'll never work," said Fangs.

Mr Nobody laughed. "Didn't you feel the rumble earlier today? That was my first test run using just three thousand hamsters. I sped up time for ninety seconds. Imagine what a million or more hamsters will do!"

"That's what happened to us at the airport,"
I said. "Time skipped forward! But you can't do it.
Billions of people will have their lives cut short."

"So?" Mr Nobody sneered. "What is important
is that someone invents the necessary machine to
return me to my body, and quickly."

"Well, I won't stand for it," Claret said. "It's
not up to you to decide how quickly other people
live their lives. If you want to continue with this
wicked scheme, you'll have to get through me
first."

"And me!" said Fangs, stepping up to stand
beside his dad.

"Me too," I said, falling into line.

"Me as well!" said Cube, joining us and
accidentally knocking his head against mine.
"Sorry," he said. "Not used to this new shape yet."

Mr Nobody sighed hard. "So be it," he said.
"I was going to allow you all to live out the rest
of your lives – albeit at a greatly increased pace.

But after that little display, I've changed my mind. Cube's usefulness is at an end, Enigma and the werewolf are annoying me – and I can't take looking at whatever it is that old bloke is wearing one moment longer."

"Now, look here—" Claret protested.

"Bring me a ball!" Nobody shouted.

A team of three skeletons ran to take up places at various workstations around the cavern and set to work operating buttons and levers. Alarms blared and lights flashed as the giant drill bit was lifted out of its hole.

Two of the Bone Boys opened up the crate again and began to spray the hamsters inside with Cube's heat-resistant liquid. There was a huge tank of it just inside the door to the laboratory.

Meanwhile, a sixth skeleton turned a handle to lower one of the giant balls from the ceiling. He opened a circular door in its side, and then pushed us inside.

Cube shook his square head in dismay. "I'm sorry," he said. "This is my fault."

"No, it's not," said Claret. "You didn't ask to be kidnapped by this ectoplasmic egotist. He's abused your skills to get his own way."

"And get my own way, I shall!" Nobody beamed. "But first – another test run. Let's use six thousand hamsters this time. The temperature at the earth's core is near to six thousand degrees Celsius, so this plastic ball will melt away almost immediately – as will anything which isn't coated in heat-resistant spray, such as yourselves. After you have burned to a crisp, I shall issue a command via a radio link, and my beautiful hamsters will begin to run as one. Time will speed up again."

The skeletons rolled the ball over so that the opening was facing the roof of the cavern. We all fell over. As we were scrambling to our feet again, 6,000 still-wet-from-being-sprayed hamsters were dumped on top of us. I could feel the weight of them pressing down on me. My nostrils twitched at the stench. I hoped it was the smell of Cube's spray and not hamster wee.

"We have to find a way out of here," Fangs gasped as the lid of the ball was screwed back in place.

"Be seeing you!" called Mr Nobody. "Oh, that's right – no, I won't."

Then his skeletons pushed the giant hamster ball into the hole and we fell towards the very centre of the planet.

As we tumbled into the darkness, the light at the top of the hole suddenly looked like a screaming mouth. I had to think fast, otherwise we wouldn't stop falling until we reached the fires at the centre of the earth.

"Fangs!" I cried. "Do a star jump."

"What?"

"DO A STAR JUMP!"

My boss clambered to his feet – which wasn't easy with his hands fastened behind his back and 6,000 hamsters crawling over him. He jumped. As he did so, I kicked him as hard as I could in the bottom.

"OW!"

The telescopic chair legs of Cube's Seat-of-Your-Pants gadget exploded out of Fangs's trousers. The ends broke through the plastic ball and embedded themselves in the wall of the hole. We came to a violent halt. The ball rocked back and forth, but the creaking legs held us in place. We had fallen around 300 metres into the hole. The hamsters scurried around the bottom of the ball, squeaking with fear.

"No one make any sudden movements," I hissed.

"Well, I'm hardly likely to, am I?" grunted Fangs. He was pressed up against the top of the ball, his hands against the smooth curve of the plastic above him – the handcuffs had been snapped off by the impact. His legs were spread almost into the splits by the poles that were holding us in place.

"Cube!" exclaimed Claret. "Your gadgets have done it again."

"Thank you," said Cube, although he didn't sound convinced.

"We're not out of this yet, Claret," I pointed out. "The next part is up to you."

"Me?" asked the older vampire. "What can I do?"

"It's time for you to take *possession* of the situation," I said. "We need the Astounding Claret to possess someone back up there in Mr Nobody's lair and operate the machinery to winch us back out."

"But I can't—" protested Claret.

"You have to," I interrupted. "No more excuses. It's our only hope of not dying a very painful death."

"I don't mean I won't do it," Claret said. "I mean I can't possess anyone up there. Mr Nobody is a ghost, and his henchmen are all skeletons."

"You could always possess one of these hamsters," suggested Fangs. "Maybe then you could climb back up the wall and save us that way."

I shook my head. "There's no way a hamster could operate the winch controls."

"There is someone else," said Cube. "Marmalade Springs."

"No," protested Fangs. "He can't possess Marmalade."

"Why not?" I asked.

Fangs sighed. "I was going to ask her out, but I can't if she's my dad!"

"Fangs," I said sternly. "If Claret doesn't do this, the only date you'll ever go on again is a very short hot one with some flame-retardant hamsters."

My boss nodded. The Astounding Claret closed his eyes, then began to tremble – and then he fell back to lie limply among the hamsters.

"Is that it?" asked Cube. "Has he done it?"

"Yes," exclaimed Fangs with pride. "Look – there's my dad."

A ghostly figure in a vampire cape was floating up towards the hole in the floor of the cavern above us.

"Oh, I wish I had a computer," moaned Cube. "I could hack into Nobody's CCTV system and watch what's going on."

"I think I can go one better, professor," I said. "But first I've got to get out of these." I twisted my wrists against the skeletal handcuffs until I heard the **SNAP!** of bones breaking. I then helped to free the professor.

"I left the Bat 'n' Ball parked behind the door in the laboratory, just in case," I explained, flying the gadget high into the air using the controls on my Smartphone. The professor and I sat among the wriggling hamsters and watched the action up above on the tiny screen.

"What's happening?" asked Fangs, who was still suspended awkwardly near the top of the ball.

"I can see your dad!" I cried. "He's sneaking up on Marmalade..." It felt strange to be saying that with Claret's body lying next to us – but I knew that was just an empty shell for the time being.

The real Claret was a few hundred metres above us, working to save our lives.

The ghostly form of Claret took up position behind Marmalade. He closed his eyes, took a deep breath – and started to step forward... Only for Mr Nobody to spot him!

"Oh no you don't!" Nobody cried, swinging round with an ectoplasmic fist. I expected it to go right through Claret, but it didn't. It hit him square in the jaw and sent him sprawling backwards across the room.

"Ghosts can make contact with other ghosts!" Cube exclaimed. "Who knew?"

As quick as a flash, Claret was back on his feet – well, hovering a few centimetres above the floor, anyway. He threw himself at Mr Nobody and wrestled him to the ground. Then he returned the punch with one of his own.

Three skeletons rushed at Claret. The see-through vampire turned and ran – or, at least,

he tried to. He clearly wasn't used to moving around without a solid body, and his feet swept through the air a few times before he was finally able to move. He wasn't fast enough, however, and the skeletons pounced – only to fall straight through him. They shattered into a pile of bones.

"Get Marmalade out of here!" Mr Nobody screamed. "I don't want him anywhere near her."

Two of the Bone Boys grabbed Marmalade and dragged her away. The only person up there who Claret could possess had gone.

Nobody peered down at us. "So, you found a way to delay your doom," he cried, squinting at the Seat-of-Your-Pants gadget. "Well, you haven't extended your pathetic lives for very long." He turned to his skeletal henchmen. "Fill another ball with hamsters and send it down on top of them."

I heard the whirr of machinery as another of the giant plastic balls was winched down from the ceiling of the cavern. I turned the Bat 'n' Ball round to see a skeleton opening a crate of hamsters. Another Bone Boy picked up the hose and began to spray the animals with Cube's potion.

122

Fangs glanced down at me in terror. "If he drops another ball on top of us..."

"...It'll dislodge us from the sides of the hole and send us plummeting to the centre of the earth," I finished.

"I think this is it," said Cube, hugging me. "I can't see a way out of this."

Then the microphone in the Bat 'n' Ball picked up a new voice. "Drop everything, Nobody! The game's up. You're under arrest."

"That ... that sounded like Mr Nobody," I said.

"He really has lost it if he's arresting himself," Fangs said.

"Do as I say, Nobody, and nobody gets hurt! Apart from Nobody, that is..." the voice went on. "The Astounding Claret is here."

"Claret has possessed Mr Nobody's body," I exclaimed.

"What?" cried Fangs.

I stared at my phone in amazement. Staggering clumsily out of the ice room, surrounded by clouds of freezing air, was the dead body of Mr Nobody.

The real Mr Nobody — the shimmering ghostly one — almost exploded with fury. "What are you doing with my body?" he screamed, his eye twitching like crazy.

"I'm possessing it," replied Claret, lumbering

forward. "It's very hard to do, and it takes lots of concentration and years of practice!"

Mr Nobody's eyes grew wide. "Teach me how to do it!" he begged. "Then I could return to my body today."

"No can do," said Claret. "You can't possess yourself – that would be ridiculous. Besides, I really don't think you want this body any more..."

"Why not?"

"It's been in the deep freeze for too long," said Claret. "It feels a bit brittle to me..." As if to prove what he was saying, there was a sickening

CRACK!

and the body's right ankle snapped off.

"You broke my foot!" screeched Mr Nobody.

"It's not just the foot, I'm afraid," Claret said. "Other bits are starting to give out too. I reckon this body will only last a matter of minutes. Still, that's long enough to save my son and his friends."

I manoeuvred the Bat 'n' Ball so we could watch Claret limp over to the winch controls and pull on a lever. A chain clattered down the hole towards us. Two of the Bone Boys dashed to stop him.

"Don't go near him," Mr Nobody ordered. "That body is the only one I've got. I don't want you clumsy oafs smashing me to pieces."

The chain knocked into the plastic ball. It had a large hook on the end. I handed the phone to Cube, then climbed up Fangs's back to sit on his shoulders. "Nearly there, boss," I said, unscrewing the lid above him.

"Thank goodness," sighed Fangs. "I could do with a good sit-down after this."

"Easily done, Agent Enigma," said Cube from below us. "I could install those chair legs in all your trousers."

"Actually, scrap that," said Fangs. "I'll be a standing-up kind of guy from now on."

I attached the hook to a fastening next to
the door in the ball. "WE'RE READY, CLARET!"
I shouted. "BRING US UP!"

I heard the winch begin to retract, and, finally,
the ball started to rise. Fangs pressed the button
to retract the chair legs and collapsed to the floor.
We gathered around the phone again so we could
watch what was going on via the Bat 'n' Ball.

Claret was pulling hard on the lever
which controlled the winch. Then—

CRACK!

His wrist snapped.

"Forget what I said!" screeched the ghost of
Mr Nobody. "Get that idiot out of my body before
he destroys it."

The Bone Boys advanced on Claret. He snatched
up the broken-off hand and jammed it into the
control panel, wedging the lever in position.

"That's my dad," said Fangs with a proud smile.

The hole above us was growing larger and larger by the second. We would be at the surface very soon.

"Now, now," Claret said to the assortment of angry and misshapen skeletons hobbling towards him. "Stay back or the body gets it!"

Mr Nobody howled with rage. "I can't watch this any more."

"Then don't," exclaimed a female voice.

Mr Nobody spun round – just as we reached the surface. We were able to watch without the aid of the Bat 'n' Ball as Marmalade Springs doused Nobody with Cube's heat-resistant cooking spray. "This should obscure your vision," she cried.

The spray hit Mr Nobody full in the face. But instead of passing through him as you'd expect, the liquid began to fill him up.

"Oh dear," cried Cube as I helped him out of the giant hamster ball. "It's the ground-up pebbles I used in the mixture. The liquid is turning solid as it hits him. It's building Mr Nobody a totally new body, from the inside out."

"You mean we're giving him exactly what he wants?" cried Fangs.

"I'm afraid so," Cube said.

Marmalade shrieked and dropped the hose, which was just as well, as Nobody was now full to the brim with sloshing, pink liquid.

"I feel amazing," he roared. "Destroy my old, inferior body if you will. This is the new me. With this stone body, I shall be more powerful than ever!"

The door to the tunnel burst open and two dozen witches flew in on broomsticks. They whizzed around the

room, hurling weighted nets over the Bone Boys.

129

Feline Scamper leapt off the back of one of the broomsticks and ran over to me.

"You arrived in the nick of time," I said with a smile. "But how did you get past the DNA lock?"

Kora the witch flew over us and dropped a bone club into my open paws. It was the weapon Claret had tossed out to sea. "One of the Bone Boys gave us a hand." Feline grinned. "You're going to prison, Nobody!" he sneered as one of the witches clamped a hand down on Nobody's shoulder. Yes, his shoulder. Mr Nobody's new body was finally complete!

Mr Nobody shrugged the witch off easily and made a break for it. Claret launched himself at Nobody, but the ghost was ready. He snatched up a wrench from the control desk and raised it above his head, preparing to strike Claret.

"NOOOO!" yelled Fangs. He pulled out the Spookie award from under his cloak and hurled it at Mr Nobody.

130

The statue hit the ghost in the back, knocking him into Claret, and the pair fell into the drill hole. The Spookie skittered away across the floor.

The award forgotten, Fangs lunged for his dad, clutching hold of the fingers of Nobody's shattered corpse. "Don't worry, Dad," Fangs cried. "I've got you!"

Only he hadn't. There was a **CRACK!** and Fangs was left holding nothing more than a detached arm.

"DAD!"

Two versions of Mr Nobody – ghostly and dead body – disappeared towards the earth's core.

"He's gone," Fangs croaked. "He saved us all, and now he's gone."

I just didn't know what to say.

"He could really do everything he said he could," Fangs continued. "And I never got to say thank you."

There was a groan behind us. The body of Claret Enigma was still inside the plastic ball with the hamsters. It sat up. "Now, what on earth possessed the Astounding Claret to think doing that was a good idea?" he asked.

CASE CLOSED
SIGNED: Agent Puppy Brown

The audience in the ballroom of the
Dorchester Hotel applauded as Phlem slid up to the
microphone. "Thank you, ladies and gentlemen," he
gurgled. "And welcome back to the concluding part
of this year's Spookie Awards ceremony."

Fangs Enigma, who was seated near the front
of the room, crossed his fingers. "This time," he
said, more to himself than to anyone else. "This
time..."

"I'm rooting for you, handsome," said Skylar,
kissing the vampire's cheek.

"As am I, son," said Claret Enigma. The older
vampire was dressed in a new suit made from lime

green silk and covered in blue sapphires. It clashed horribly with his orange-sequined cape.

Feline Scamper winked at a werewolf sitting next to him. "Do you think he'll win one?" he asked.

"Oh, I hope so," said Puppy Brown. "Or I'll never hear the end of it."

"A bit like me back home," said Feline. "It doesn't do a cat's reputation much good to have a million or so hamsters smuggled into the country, right under his whiskers! Still, it's a free pet for every classroom in Greece."

There was more applause as a new figure took to the stage – it was Cube! He was wearing a square-shaped wooden frame over his head, as he had done ever since he had returned to London a few days earlier. Unfortunately, it was rather heavy, and he staggered slightly, bumping his now flattened forehead into the mike.

"Oops," he said, his voice echoing around the room. "I feel such a *square* – thank goodness."

"Get on with it!" barked a voice that may or may not have belonged to Fangs Enigma.

"All right, all right," said Cube, tearing open a golden envelope. "And the award for the world's greatest vampire spy goes to ... Claret Enigma!"

"WHAT?" cried Fangs. But his protestations were quickly drowned out as the rest of the room leapt to their feet in a standing ovation.

Puppy Brown watched open-mouthed as Claret jumped up from his seat, grabbed Skylar's hand and dragged her up onto the stage with him. Meanwhile, Fangs's mouth was flapping open and closed. He looked like a goldfish.

Phlem handed the award to the older vampire, who paused to slip on a pair of dark sunglasses before approaching the microphone. "The Astounding Claret truly deserves this," he exclaimed. Then he ran towards the exit, dragging his new date with him.

"Dad," shouted Fangs, "get back here right now!"

Claret didn't even glance over his shoulder.

"Dad! DAD!"

"Here we go again." Puppy Brown smiled before racing out of the room after her vampire boss and best friend, Fangs Enigma.

ABOUT THE AUTHOR

TOMMY DONBAVAND was born and brought up in Liverpool and has worked at numerous careers that have included clown, actor, theatre producer, children's entertainer, drama teacher, storyteller and writer. He is the author of the popular thirteen-book series Scream Street. His other books include *Zombie!*; *Wolf*; *Uniform*; and Doctor Who: *Shroud of Sorrow*. His non-fiction books for children and their parents, *Boredom Busters* and *Quick Fixes for Bored Kids*, have helped him to become a regular guest on radio stations around the UK and he also writes for a number of magazines, including *Creative Steps* and Scholastic's *Junior Education*.

Tommy lives in Lancashire with his family.

He is a huge fan of all things Doctor Who, plays blues harmonica and makes a mean balloon poodle.

He sees sleep as a waste of good writing time.

You can find out more about Tommy and his books at his website: www.tommydonbavand.com

Visit the Fangs website at: www.fangsvampirespy.co.uk

TEST YOUR SECRET-AGENT

Spot the Difference (There are eight to spot.)

SKILLS WITH THESE PUZZLES!

Mr Nobody Facts

How well do you know this book?
Answer these questions and find out!

1) What is Fangs's dad called?

2) What type of animal is Agent Feline Scamper?

3) Can you name a gadget used in this book? (Get a bonus point if you can name more than one!)

Mr Nobody Facts

Claret Enigma; a cat; Bat 'n' Ball, heat-resistant cooking spray, Sticky Soap and Seat of Your Pants.

Answers

UNLOCK SECRET MISSION FILES!

Want to gain access to highly classified MPl files?

Find the code word hidden in the square

below and enter it at

WWW.FANGSVAMPIRESPY.CO.UK/MISSION4

Which Fangs character is this?

```
T  A  T  R
L        E
E        R
L  C  C  A
```

— — — — — —

(Hint: all the letters appear twice. Cross out one of each pair.
Six letters should then remain in the box.
Reorder these to find the secret word!)